Judge Benjamin: THE SUPERDOG GIFT

Judith Whitelock McInerney

DRAWINGS BY *Leslie Morrill*

Troll Associates

for MY GIFTS—
SHAMUS
KELLY
JENNIFER
MEGAN

A TROLL BOOK, published by Troll Associates,
Mahwah, NJ 07430

Published by arrangement with Holiday House. For information address Holiday House, 18 East 53rd Street, New York, New York 10022.

First Troll Printing, 1987

Printed in the United States of America

10 9 8 7 6 5 4 3 2 1

ISBN 0-8167-1043-0

Chapter 1

Agatha Bliss could sleep until noon. She lay curled on the back step, breathing heavily in a deep, dreamy Saint Bernard sleep.

As much as we both loved the brisk cold and snow of December in Decatur, Illinois, I was grateful for this week of unseasonably mild nights. Agatha and I were enjoying some private evenings outside together.

I'm Judge Benjamin, the two-hundred-pound Saint Bernard who takes care of the crazy O'Riley household. Maggie and Tom O'Riley and their four children—Seth, Kathleen, Annie Elizabeth, and Maura—combine fun and work the way most big families do. Agatha became part of the family just a few weeks ago. The strange disappearance of her owner and our own good fortune brought her to us. We both feel lucky to be part of this family.

I watched Agatha for several minutes as a warm sunrise pushed its glow through the morning sky. I could hardly remember what it was like before we found her. She had been so thin and frail living alone in the country, but now she was beautiful, content, and healthy.

I heard Annie Elizabeth at the back door protesting her job as "garbage-taker-outer."

"But I'm ony free years old," she said. "Free-year-olds shouldna oughta do big jobs."

"Hmmm. Just yesterday you told me you were getting so big you thought you should have your ears pierced," Maggie said smoothly.

There was a brief silent pause. Tom's hand pushed open the back door. His other hand patted Annie's shoulder as she stepped outside carrying a big brown bag. Tom whispered something in her ear, and her martyred frown melted into a big smile. Annie turned to smile at Tom, but she kept walking—and stepped right on Agatha's ear. When Annie jumped back, a layer of garbage tumbled out of the bag.

"I'm sorry, Agafa."

Annie forgot Tom, and instead of being a bag lady, she became a nurse.

"Did I hurt you, pooo ting?" Annie made a major ordeal out of petting and pouting.

Agatha opened one eye, sighed quietly, and went back to sleep. A long-suffering sigh was a Saint Bernard standard. I used it often myself.

Annie walked over to me. "Best she just rest, huh, Judge?" she said. "She's a late getter-upper anyways."

I nudged her hand in approval. Annie had that right. I was in the habit of taking mini-naps throughout the day, but Agatha liked a late morning sleep.

Annie spent several minutes picking up a gooey tomato soup can, some wet paper towels, and a dirty doughnut box. Then she opened the door to go back inside. "You comin', Judge?"

I could smell jelly doughnuts, and decided to follow.

Annie forgot the brown bag. Instead of finding its way into the can near the fence, it remained on the step beside Agatha. Next guy out the back door was in for a surprise.

In the kitchen, Seth was filling out his spelling notebook, and Kathleen was wiping strawberry jelly spots off its spiral binding.

"You know you're not supposed to do your homework at the table," Kathleen scolded. "Why don't you do it after school like everybody else in the family?"

The only other everybody else with homework was Kathleen. The message wasn't lost on Seth, but he decided not to dignify her question with an answer. He just solemnly clicked the corner of his mouth. He did it a second time for good measure and kept his head in the book.

I wish I could do that, but something gets lost in the thick skin of my jowls.

Tom walked in wearing his favorite blue blazer, striped shirt, silk tie, socks, and shiny shoes. The color coordination stopped at his waist since he sported only underwear on his bottom half.

"Maggie, didn't my gray trousers come back from the cleaners?" he asked.

"Front hall closet." Maggie looked up from the bacon she was frying long enough to smile. "Of course, you'll be much more impressive to those bankers if you go like that."

Seth looked up and whistled. "Yeah, wow. Great legs."

Tom heard the giggles as he left the room. He came back in waving his shirttail like a cancan

dancer swirling her ruffled crinolines. He spun around and bowed. After a few more giggles, he left again in search of his pants.

Maggie handed Annie a small brown bag filled with sugar to shake on the doughnuts. Kathleen was taking the doughnuts out of the oven and passing them along to Annie, a few at a time.

I parked under Maura's highchair. The floor underneath was already generously sprinkled with wet Froot Loops and toast crusts.

I made myself useful and cleaned up the leavings. Not too bad—she'd left just enough orange marmalade to give the bread zip.

I was thinking how good it would taste to wash the final scraps down with milk when Maura obliged by turning over her Tommy Tippee. A cold white milkfall rained on my nose.

Seth looked up from his spelling book and made a grab for the cup. But he only managed to knock the butter dish off the table.

Annie came over to investigate, dropping to her knees. As she bent, so did the brown bag, and a sugar mountain grew on my paw.

Kathleen moved in. *"Annie!"* Kathleen moaned. She set the bag down long enough for Seth to sneak the doughnuts out of their frosty hideaway and into his mouth.

I could hardly blame him. They smelled so good, Maggie never could keep them around long.

"Seth!" Kathleen recognized two pudgy cheeks for what they were. Doughnut caves. "Save some for the rest of us."

Tom came back into the kitchen, this time with his pants on. "Settle down, kids." He walked right past the mess and sat down.

Maggie made a full turn from the frying pan, waving a hot spatula. "Tom, look what *your* children did this morning."

She said it playfully enough, but Tom caught the hint. He took paper towels, a broom, and a dustpan, and tackled the mess.

Tom took his time. That way he could be sure no one would give him any other jobs. Seth put his spelling away long enough to slice some bananas and pour cream into a pitcher. Maggie brought the bacon, eggs, and what doughnuts she had managed to guard to the table. Kathleen pulled out Annie's chair and plunked her in it. Maura was still in her highchair cooing at the floor where her milk had disappeared.

Everyone waited for Tom. He stood up, handing the broom to Maggie. He grabbed a dish towel and waved the still full dustpan like a dancer poising a fan. He began a strange two-step toward the back door to empty the sugar mess.

A pirouette.

A "Ta-Ta."

Then more of the cancan.

He sang dreadfully off key:

So . . . kick as high as you can
when you do the cancan . . .

It was sooooo bad. Maggie and Seth and Kathleen clapped the beat to drown him out.

But he kept it up.

. . . come on out and show us how it goes . . .

With that, Tom cancanned out the back door —right into Annie's garbage! A pair of polished wing tips appeared, heel side up, on the other side of the glass storm door. A very surprised Tom had landed on the sleeping body of a very surprised Agatha.

She opened both eyes this time, on a typical O'Riley morning.

Chapter 2

It was close, but Tom made it to work on time, and Seth and Kathleen caught their bus on the run.

No one had been able to stop laughing long enough to clean up the kitchen.

When Tom walked out the front door, he had eleven water spots on his clothes where he had tried to rinse off splotches of tomato soup and old food. He said he'd drive fast and blow-dry.

Seth and Kathleen put the doughnuts that no one had time to eat in their lunch bags, and Maggie put Maura in the playpen with Annie. Annie objected but Maggie insisted, and soon

Annie was performing her version of the Sleeping Beauty to a wide-eyed Maura.

Maggie fed Agatha and me in the kitchen while she hummed and puttered her way through the breakfast mess. The teakettle she had put on the back burner perked just as she shut the dishwasher door on the last plate.

Our breakfast was dinner revisited: microwave-warmed gravy, cornbread, and scalloped potatoes, mixed with our daily ration of Gainesburgers.

Agatha and I each had our own bowl. My huge dented saucepan had seen better days, but the flowers and hearts that Annie had carefully painted on it one Valentine's Day made it special.

Agatha used a big aluminum punch bowl that in its heyday had graced First Communions, wedding receptions, and church suppers. Maggie set it too close to the Weber grill once and the heat from the charcoal curved its lip. Now it looked like a queen-sized gravy bowl, which, in fact, it had become. Annie would probably personalize it one of these days, too.

I finished first, as usual.

Maggie sat down in her chair with a cup of tea, patting me and talking to us both. "I can always count on you two appreciating my cooking—even the day after."

She waited patiently until Agatha slurped the last crumb.

"Good girl, Agatha. We'll get healthy weight on you yet," Maggie said.

No one ever said that to me. I was never without healthy weight. My problem was pounds off, not pounds on. But Maggie was right to be concerned about Agatha. Poor Agatha had barely managed to survive the days when her first owner, Mrs. Ardella Hoffman, had gotten sick.

I looked at Agatha as she sat down near Maggie, putting a paw next to Maggie's lap. She was filling out nicely now. Maggie's cooking was working wonders.

"Either of you guys want a doughnut? I sneaked these aside before the kids saw them." Maggie took one step up the stool and got a covered plate from the back of the top of the refrigerator.

I needed no encouragement. Agatha sensed that Maggie wanted her to have some, so she obliged, too.

The ring of the phone and a cry from Maura sounded at the same time. Maggie hesitated before answering but decided Maura could wait.

"Why, Carol Hoffman Clint, how nice to hear from you," Maggie said.

The name of Carol Hoffman Clint, the daughter of Agatha's former owner, was a little too interesting to ignore.

". . . in town? Oh, I'd be disappointed if you didn't . . ."

I don't know why, but a funny tingle crept up my back. Why would Carol come here?

When Maggie finally hung up the phone, her face wore that "I'd better work fast" look.

She found a basket, filled it with fresh fruit from the fridge, lit the pine-scented candle on the coffee table, and swatted a cobweb off the dining room light fixture. Then she picked up a fussy Maura and announced to Annie: "Let's get dolled up, kids. We're having company."

I didn't have to ask who was coming to dinner.

Chapter 3

Carol Hoffman Clint arrived, not for dinner, but for lunch.

Maggie was still pulling the electric rollers out of her hair when the doorbell rang. Maura and Annie were spiffy and smiling, but Maggie's silk blouse could have used a touch-up with an iron, and her finger-combed hair left something to be desired. Especially since the woman on the other side of the door rated a ten and a half.

Carol, tall and striking, wore a rusty suede split skirt and high-heeled boots. A jaunty angora beret hid most of her very short, very chic red hair. In contrast to her stylish image, a huge old truck with the words SALEM SAM—WE BUY AND SELL sat in the driveway.

Carol stepped inside, shook Maggie's hand firmly, quickly hugged Maura and Annie, then gave a good, long hug to Agatha. "Aggie, you gorgeous dame!"

Dame? It didn't seem to fit, but Agatha was loving it. I could see that even though Carol's job of supplying her boutique business called for frequent travel, she'd managed enough trips back to her mother's home to form a warm bond with Agatha.

Carol stepped back and gave me the once-over.

"And this is the gorgeous-hunk-knight-in-shining-armor Judge Benjamin?"

Hunk? Well, maybe she got that right. A guy could hope.

Maggie liked Carol right away. We all did. She was one of those people who gave you no good reason not to.

"Take your coat?" Maggie reached for Carol's tweed jacket, but Carol had already deposited it on the nearest doorknob. She sat down on the floor near Agatha and pulled Maura toward her lap.

"Gorgeous kids. Just gorgeous," she said.

Maura took that as a cue to gurgle and coo wildly.

"You didna come to take Agafa away, did you?" Annie's voice cracked a bit.

I was a little afraid of the answer.

"Are you kidding?" Carol put our fears to rest. "This is Agatha's new home, and Mom and I both know she is very lucky to have it."

Annie was quiet. She sat on my paw and leaned against my shoulder.

"Tea or coffee?" Maggie asked on her way to the kitchen.

"Tea, thanks. Got any of that low-calorie sweetener?" Carol dug into her huge tote bag and found some toffee. She passed it to Annie.

Maggie put the water on and came back into the living room. "I hope you have some good news about Ardella. Does she really understand about Agatha's new home? We've wondered . . ."

Carol jostled Maura on her knee. "It's as good as the news can be. She has good days and bad days. On the good days, it hardly seems anything is wrong at all. That's the way with Alzheimer's disease. But the hard part is she can't be left alone. Not at all. Because there is no way to predict the bad days."

"But with your job . . ." Maggie answered the whistling teakettle and came back with the tea.

"Well, that's part of the good news," Carol said. "We found a senior care center an hour and a half from our home with a marvelously flexible program."

Annie was leaning forward now with her head propped in her hands. She looked a bit puzzled, but she didn't interrupt.

Carol put Maura on the floor by me and went on with her story. "The home's policy allows for visitors at any time, and an authorized guardian can sign a patient out for weekends or special days. When I'm in town, she stays with me. When I'm not, she's at the center full-time. It's really wonderful."

Maggie set a plate of cookies on the coffee table. "Annie, would you bring the plate of sandwiches from the fridge?"

Annie knew exactly what plate Maggie meant because Maggie had let her put olive faces on the chicken salad.

Maggie waited till Annie was out of earshot. "Carol, about Agatha . . . would it help Ardella to have her back? We really love her, but . . ."

Carol put her cup down.

That tingle kept returning to my back. I

looked at Agatha. She was sitting very straight, watching me.

"Maggie, Agatha was the sweetest, most loyal friend my mother could have ever hoped to have. So many times when my mother wandered off and could have gotten into trouble, Agatha was right beside her, helping. But that last time, when my mother managed to board a bus to parts unknown, there was just no way Agatha could continue to protect her. Mother needs different kinds of friends now. She needs doctors and nurses, and Agatha needs a new life." Carol smoothed Agatha's fur. Her kindness seemed to stretch through her fingers to Agatha.

Annie walked in, tilting the sandwiches at a dangerous angle. Maggie rescued the plate.

"In fact," Carol went on, "that's really why I've come. These belong with Agatha."

Carol dumped the entire contents of her huge tote bag on the living room floor. She picked up a big blue album and handed it to Annie. She made a neat pile of leashes and toys and set them in front of Agatha. Then she handed Maggie a manila folder.

"Papers," Carol said. "Vet records, pedigree—I thought you would want them. She comes from champion bloodlines, but there may be a little problem with puppies."

That was simple enough language for Annie to understand.

"Puppies? Thas no problem. I'll take care of 'em," she volunteered.

"I'm sure you would," Carol said, smiling, "but a few years back Agatha had a problem with pylometra, an infection . . ."

Annie's face went blank again. Puppies she understood. Big words she didn't.

The big words *I* could handle, but puppies?

Annie started feeding me sandwiches to take her mind off what she didn't understand. Chicken salad, with water chestnuts. My head began to clear as my stomach filled.

Annie passed one to Agatha, and Maggie moved the plate.

"You mean she can't . . ." Maggie poured some more tea.

"It's a maybe," Carol said, shrugging her shoulders.

Maura had toddled over to the teapot, but Agatha nudged her in the other direction. Maura found the cookie plate instead.

"We have an appointment for both the Saints next week. The vet will appreciate these old records. You were so thoughtful to bring them." Maggie looked a bit worried, but she said no more about it.

"Ah, but that's not my best gift," Carol said. "I've got something you're going to love."

"Is it a big word?" Annie asked a little shyly.

Carol laughed. "I think you can handle this one. When we sold my mother's house, I saved a few things from the hand of the auctioneer. I can restore some for resale in my boutique, but for you—well, come on out. I've saved something special for Agatha and Judge."

Maggie scooped Maura onto her hip, and we all went out to the front of the house.

The truck was absolutely, positively packed. Boxes, chests, and trunks were wedged into every nook and cranny, peeking from the sides and corners of the too-small tarp that should have covered them. Carol scaled first the fender, then the heap, carefully folding back the cover like a neat diaper and hanging it on the back of the cab.

There, taking up two-thirds of the truck bed, sat a full-sized, six-passenger sleigh!

Carol stood with one high-heeled foot in a box of trophies and the other balanced on the sleigh seat. "Well, what do you think? Dad had it made for our Shetland pony, but with a double harness, the two Saints could pull it easily!"

Carol looked absolutely joyful, but Maggie looked doubtful.

Carol kept talking. "It was in the old shed. Oh, the memories I have! The kids will love it."

Annie, the kid of the moment, got wide-eyed.

"I really appreciate this . . ." Maggie said uncertainly. "Why don't I call Tom home for lunch and we can get this thing unloaded?"

Something about the way Maggie said the word "thing" smacked of ingratitude.

Carol shot her one of those very liberated female looks. "*We* can get this unloaded. Now."

"Of course we can," Maggie said. She was trying to convince herself not only that they could manage it, but that she wanted to.

"Sam's truck has a power-lift tailgate," Carol explained. "He installed it himself, and he says a ten-year-old can handle it. I'm sure that's right because even when we graduated from high school together, he impressed me as something of a ten-year-old."

Maggie took a deep breath. She put Maura on the ground by the crab apple tree and asked Annie to keep an eye on her.

Carol was still talking, taking boxes from the top of the sleigh and lining them up in the driveway. Since the sleigh was flush to the back of the truck, it didn't take her long.

"Sam said the mechanism on the lift sticks once in a while, so I'll stay by the button in the cab and you keep an eye on the back. Just hang on to the sleigh rail and guide it a bit and tell me when to stop the lift, O.K.?"

Agatha was walking around the front of the truck, taking everything in. I followed her. It was more fun than watching the pained expression on Maggie's reluctant face.

It was some truck. It had every kind of extra imaginable, including red racing stripes.

Carol was still giving directions to Maggie. "See, you just steer it so it doesn't slide too far to one side. The lift does all the work. I'll get in the cab and get things going."

Carol started the engine. Apparently nothing worked without it. It was noisy and vibrated steadily. "All set?" she yelled back to Maggie.

Maggie appeared to be anything but all set, but she answered yes anyway.

Carol could barely hear her. When she looked out the window, all she could see was the tarp hanging on the back of the cab. She opened the driver's door and looked around. Satisfied, she hit the button for the power lift.

The lift creaked and groaned and whirred, but slowly it began to move. Maggie put one hand on the side of the sleigh to keep it straight. Maura fell down and started to cry.

"It's O.K., I got 'er," Annie yelled.

But the noise of the lift and the engine drowned both sounds out. The lift kept going down, down, speeding up a bit and easing the sleigh toward the driveway.

Maura was crying harder. Annie began scolding her, and Carol looked around to see what was causing all the commotion. Meanwhile, Maggie began waving frantically.

"Carol," she shouted, "you can stop it now, Carol, you better . . ."

Carol was hearing the wrong signals. Annie was telling Maura, "C'mon, that's good . . ." while Maggie was screaming, *"Carol!"*

Suddenly the cab of the truck began to lift up. The weight of the sleigh was pulling the back down. The more it tilted, the more Maggie screamed.

"Maggie?" Carol looked at the driveway, which was getting farther away.

I didn't know how much worse things could get, but I did know that the load in front needed to be as heavy as the load in back.

I jumped in the open cab door. Agatha was right behind me. Poor Carol was somewhere underneath us. But she finally hit the button!

Chapter 4

The look on Tom's face when he discovered the huge sleigh standing on its side with one broken runner and a punctured seat was a classic.

But so was Maggie's explanation. "Minor shipping damage."

She didn't elaborate, and he didn't ask her to. They'd been married long enough to understand that there are some things you're better off not knowing.

Cold weather, Christmas lights downtown, and carols on the radio brought thoughts of Christmas. Carol's gift of the sleigh spurred visions of sugarplums, so just days after she left, we made plans to buy our Christmas tree.

The mood was perfect. Well, almost perfect.

"I'm so mad," Annie said, racing into the kitchen, where everyone had gathered near the coatrack. "We shoulda had snow. We shoulda. Then we could take Judge and Agafa and the sleigh . . ."

"Now, hold on, Annie. If we took the sleigh, we couldn't *all* go pick out the tree. Remember, it holds a maximum of six passengers. Now, who would we leave in the forest so the tree could ride home?" Tom asked.

"Seth." Annie said it without blinking.

Seth feigned heartbreak, rolling on the floor, sobbing.

"You really are going to be a smart one, Annie." Kathleen was laughing. "Able to know instantly the difference between quality and quantity."

Kathleen tried to put Maura's mittens on, but every time she got close, Maura made an impossibly fat fist.

Seth got up off the floor. "Hey, Maura, how big are you?"

Instinctively, Maura raised her hands straight to the ceiling. Kathleen moved in with one mitten. "Thanks. One more?"

Seth obliged. He asked again, "So big?"

Maura's hands went back up, and Kathleen scooted the other mitten on.

Maura decided to get even bigger. She pulled herself up with the help of Agatha's ear and raised one leg. But the other leg wasn't quite reliable enough to hold her enthusiastically waving limbs. She plopped down neatly on the softest part of her. Then she changed the game to "how little." She lay down. She got tired of that but couldn't make it back to a sitting position because of her thick down snowsuit. Agatha heard her whine and looked around. She pushed Maura back into a sit. It was nice to have Agatha's instinctive help.

"I'm glad it's not snowing," Maggie said. "If we brought home a snow-covered tree, we'd have to wait at least a day for the needles to dry before we could decorate it."

"What is the forecast?" Tom asked, pulling on his shearling coat. "It's gotten pretty cold after those few mild days."

"I'd say you just have time to repair the sleigh runner before a maiden voyage." Maggie was tying scarves and checking zippers on Annie and Maura. "If you start right now—after the tree . . ."

Tom groaned and led the way to the car.

I had been afraid Tom might not want Agatha and me along for the ride. Even in the station wagon, there wasn't much room once you added a Christmas tree, but he opened the back door and whistled as we jumped inside. The rest of the family piled in, filling the front and back seats.

Good enough. I hoped if something had to be tied on the roof for the ride home, it wouldn't be me.

Halfway to the tree farm in Taylorville, Tom remembered the leashes.

"Rats, Maggie. The last time we brought the Judge, that man almost wouldn't let us in," Tom said.

"I remember," Maggie answered. "He said we had to contain our 'wild beast' or leave him outside. If we hadn't found that twine . . ."

"Twine isn't going to work this time. We have two big dogs, and I think that man is on to us," Tom said.

Kathleen took off her long red wool scarf. She slipped it under Agatha's collar, looped it through, and pulled. "How's this?"

"Smashing," Maggie said. "But will it pass security?"

Seth took off his wool plaid scarf and did the

same to me. "Dashing. Reeallly!"

Tom said, "This is the plan. We march in, no hesitation, before the guy has a chance to give us grief. If that doesn't work"—Tom looked back at Agatha and me and smiled—"I want you two Saints to snarl and hiss."

Agatha and I looked at each other. Snarling was unbecoming to our breed . . . but what price Christmas spirit!

As it turned out, a lady, not a man, was handling the tree sales. She couldn't have been nicer, patting and talking to Agatha and me. Just for sport—we looked so rakish—Maggie let us keep the scarves on anyway.

It seemed as if everyone in central Illinois had picked this weekend to find a tree. The place was really crowded.

Our plan was to stick together, but the tree farm was not built for eight bodies walking side by side, particularly when Agatha and I were built like small tractors. We kept bumping into people and nearly mowing down the trees.

Tom came up with a new plan. We could go faster and probably have better luck if we divided into two groups.

"O.K.," Tom said. "How about males and

Maura on one team and everyone else on the other?"

Tom's plan lasted three trees. Then Maura began to fuss and Annie complained because Kathleen got to lead the way. We reassembled in the middle of the tree farm to decide on a "new plan."

An assortment of other people converged on the single best tree at the tree farm, which happened to be located just behind Maggie.

We all realized it at once. The perfect tree. Within reach.

Twelve voices chorused, "We'll take this one!"

A pause followed. Then some shouts of "Why?," "We saw it first," and "It's ours and that's that" filled the air.

When one large woman made her point with a swing of her huge pocketbook, it caught little Annie on the back of the head. I felt obliged to add my two cents to the argument. I barked a marvelous, thundering Saint Bernard woof, and Agatha added one of her own.

The silence was brief.

It was a case of great minds running in the same channel.

Seth threw his hand to his mouth and gasped,

"Oh, no. They're not going to start biting again!"

The O'Rileys' creativity rose with Seth's inspiration.

Kathleen picked it up. "Dad, do something—remember last time—all the blood, the crying . . . ?!" She clutched her throat and looked as if she would be very sick.

Tom grabbed our scarves, pretending to rein us in. "Maggie, you better get the little ones out of here."

Agatha and I were overcome with the spirit of the moment. I kept up a series of thumping woofs. Agatha reared on her hind legs, pawing air. It was like a scene from *Call of the Wild.*

The competition scattered. Only the O'Rileys remained.

A quiver of guilt about the charade melted when the giggles started. Just one thing mattered. We got the tree.

We expected Maggie to scold us, but we were wrong. She laughed so hard all the way home that tears came to her eyes. She kept saying, "Well, somebody had to get the perfect tree." Then she'd start laughing again.

Tom suggested that perhaps next year we should try out a new tree farm. Maybe we had worn out our welcome at that one.

"I'm just so proud of Agatha," Kathleen said. "Judge Benjamin is used to our craziness, but this is Agatha's first time ad-libbing with the family."

Agatha beamed. Dear Agatha. Funny, you don't know you miss something until you have it, and once you do . . .

"What's for dinner?" asked Seth. Naturally.

"That depends," Maggie answered. "If you want to put the perfect tree up tonight, maybe peanut butter. If you want a seven-course meal, we can put the tree up next weekend."

"Treeeeee!" everyone answered at once.

"How about pizza and tree?" Tom suggested.

"Pizza! Tree! Tree! Pizza!"

It was a noisy ride home. In fact, the volume grew throughout the evening. Putting up the O'Riley Christmas tree produced more decibels than a rock group. Agatha and I were delighted spectators at a three-ring family circus.

One catastrophe barely cleared another. Maura sat in the box of breakable ornaments. A shorted set of lights sent a spark to the carpet, but a spill from Annie's hot chocolate put the fire out. The Christmas tree stand broke, and Tom had to make a new leg for it. Kathleen nearly fell trying to put the star on top of the tree, and when Maggie ran in from the kitchen in time to catch her, the hot chocolate boiled over on the stove. That set off the smoke detectors. . . . Seth turned them off. He also turned off the other lights in the house, while Kathleen plugged in the finished tree.

Some things are worth the struggle.

Everyone fell silent. The colored lights, the traditional decorations, the gifts scattered underneath the tree, the manger on its simple straw cloth at the bottom—nothing needed to be said.

We all knew magic when we saw it. And that's what this was.

Chapter 5

When Tom was called out of town two weeks before Christmas, the same week the weatherman predicted snow, Maggie assumed the responsibility for repairing the sleigh. She assembled tools and materials, checked her busy schedule for time to complete the job, and acted on her best instincts.

She hired a carpenter. Joseph Cavato, a friend and almost neighbor, worked from a basement shop in a boardinghouse he managed. It was exactly one mile from the O'Riley house, the midpoint of Tom's two-mile morning run. On this particular Monday morning, it was to be the first of many errands, from the grocery store to the veterinarian. Shortly after Kathleen and Seth hopped the bus for school, Maggie buckled Annie and Maura in their car seats and opened the tailgate for Agatha and me.

I looked forward to the vet checkups. Dr. Baker was a great kidder. He never let us leave without Milk Bones and good wishes. Besides, I was anxious to hear if Agatha had fully recovered from her past health problems. She no longer looked frail and thin as she had when I first found her, but that business Carol mentioned bothered me. I noticed Maggie had the manila folder on the front seat of the car.

In spite of the cold of the December day, we found Mr. Cavato outside, washing his three-wheel bike. His assistant, George, was holding a hose in his mouth, aiming the running water at the right level to rinse the wheels as Mr. Cavato washed.

George had a face that would stop traffic. Never had I met an English bulldog that was more English bulldog. For some reason, the end of the gray hose reminded me of a cigar, and a picture formed in my head of George in a fireman's hat. But even without props, George looked plenty old and ugly. His looks were deceiving. George was only three years old and the sweetest dog you would ever want to meet.

Maura and Annie and Agatha and I were out of the car bothering him in no time flat. George greeted us with a slight nod of his head.

Maggie saw what was coming and ran to turn off the hose. Only a few minor sprinkles of water sprayed the area.

Maura thought it was a great game and kept picking up the hose, looking inside for more of the brief shower.

"Mr. Cavato, I've been trying to call but your line's always busy," Maggie said.

Joseph Cavato wiped his hands on his khaki pants, carefully folded the dirty rag he had been using, and gestured toward a large man sleeping on the porch swing.

"Dad. He has girlfriends most everywhere. The phone bill looks like the national debt," Joseph replied. "He's taking a rare break."

Mr. Cavato opened the porch door for all of us, despite Maggie's protests. We marched into the parlor of the grand old house, a mini-parade of dogs and people.

George moved slowly and with great effort, as if gravity played some special kind of trick on him that no one else had to endure. He lay down on a spot on the rag rug in front of the fireplace and fell asleep immediately. We never so much as saw him twitch a paw, even though Maura and Annie petted and tweaked him the whole time we were there.

The parlor was a smorgasbord of antiques, silk flowers, woodwork, and people. Like snowflakes, no two anythings were alike. We felt instantly at home.

I sat near Maggie and Mr. Cavato, listening vaguely to their conversation about fixing the sleigh. Maggie gave him the measurements of the runner, and he said he'd have a new one for us in the morning. He'd stop by to put it on after morning Mass.

Agatha did not sit down. She stood staring at the two boarders sitting on the bay window seat. A tall man with a paisley bow tie spoke softly to a tiny woman with very curly reddish hair. They were eating fudgesicles, but the woman had more drips than licks. She didn't seem to notice.

"You missed dinner again, Loretta," the man said.

Loretta began to hum. With one hand she waved her fingers as if she were playing a piano in the air. The man fidgeted with his tie and asked again, "Loretta?"

The chocolate ice cream made larger spots on Loretta's pale blue dirndl skirt.

Agatha moved in, catching the drips on her nose and licking them away. The man scooted closer to Loretta. She moved farther to the side. He tried again. He was indeed an earnest suitor, but Loretta showed no interest.

"I have to know," he said desperately. "Is there someone else?"

Loretta just looked out the window. She seemed to be a million miles away. When she finally felt the cold, wet drips oozing down her knuckles, she stared at the fudgesicle and set it down on the seat beside her.

Mr. Cavato walked over to the couple. "John, best leave Loretta be now. She'll be herself later."

Agatha was gently licking the sticky ice cream from the woman's hand. Something about the incident struck a chord in Agatha. Loretta didn't look at her but began to stroke Agatha's furry head.

Mr. Cavato handed Loretta his handkerchief and turned to Maggie. "She's leaving at the end of the month to stay with her son. We've had a little problem with her taking walks and not coming back," he explained in a whisper.

Maggie said nothing. She just watched Agatha. Something about Loretta had made Agatha think of Ardella, her first owner. Agatha did not want to leave, but Annie grabbed her thick neck and began to pull.

"C'mon, Agafa," Annie said, tugging. "We got to see about puppies."

Agatha stared for another long moment at Loretta. Then she rose patiently and followed her little leader, Annie. She looked back twice, and her eyes seemed pained.

I studied Loretta. We had seen many pictures of Ardella in the album Carol Hoffman Clint had brought us. Loretta and Ardella both had a strong jaw and strawberry hair and wide-set eyes —Loretta could have been Ardella's double. To see Loretta's lapses in mood suggested a serious health problem. Could it mean Alzheimer's disease—the same illness Ardella suffered from? It was a spooky coincidence.

Chapter 6

The fender bender caught us halfway through our errands.

A light snow had begun to fall—just enough to slicken the pavement. Maggie pulled through the green light more slowly than usual, but not slowly enough. When a young man in a jeep turned right on red in front of us, he caused a skid to crunch metal. Ours and his.

Agatha and I were sharing the back of the station wagon with nine bags of groceries, so we couldn't have gone anywhere. The groceries were like produce air bags, keeping us from sliding. Annie, Maura, and Maggie, held tight by their seat belts, were shaken but fine. The accident was a nuisance but not a disaster.

The fellow got out of his jeep, staring daggers at Maggie and muttering something about women drivers. We saw him stomping toward the car, clearly ignoring the fact that the accident had been his fault.

Maggie let Agatha and me out of the car. He stopped muttering. Annie said matter-of-factly, "You shouldn' crashed into us. Now our car's broke."

Maggie cleared her throat. "Perhaps you're not completely aware of the responsibilities inherent in the right-turn-on-red provision in the state of Illinois. . . ."

The poor guy never knew what hit him. By the time the sheriff arrived, the jeep driver was singing a more apologetic tune. He had walked to a nearby phone to order a tow. Our bumper was wrapped way under our front wheel and couldn't be pulled back without special tools. He'd called Dr. Baker to cancel our vet appointment since the accident had already made us late and Dr. Baker stuck to a very exact schedule. We'd have to reschedule when we got home. He'd called the police to report the crash, and he'd given Maggie all the insurance information she needed.

Even though he didn't do it eagerly, he did agree to drive us, and the nine bags of groceries, home. Considerable confusion followed. Maggie insisted on bringing Maura's car seat, and the one place it could be properly fastened was in the front passenger seat. With that seat occupying so much space, Annie was the only passenger who could fit in the front with the driver, so Maggie and the nine bags of groceries squeezed into the back with Agatha and me.

My neck was wedged against the roll bar and my paw felt something dripping from a brown bag that smelled distinctly like butter pecan ice cream. Agatha's head was pushed out the side tarp where a piece of plastic served as a window. She kept blinking away the snowflakes. Maggie balanced three bags of groceries on her lap and didn't dare breathe.

We watched our car being towed away and wondered how we'd manage without wheels for the rest of the week. Tom wouldn't be back till Friday.

It had been a peculiar day. Agatha had been very quiet throughout the ordeal, and it worried me. I had become used to the hectic life of a family, but Agatha had come from something quite different. It occurred to me that maybe she wasn't as happy as I was.

My paw was now nearly covered with the brown, sticky ice cream. Well, thank goodness we had at least gotten groceries. I began licking it, but the sticky feeling stayed between my claws.

At least nothing more could happen. We'd be home soon, Seth and Kathleen would be back from school, and the day would be behind us. Or so I thought. Within seconds, Agatha jumped—a powerful lunge out of the jeep just as the driver slowed to a yield sign.

Agatha?

It caught us all by surprise. Maggie and I were wedged against the groceries and couldn't have followed that jump if we'd tried.

It was Annie who screamed. "Agafa! Where you go?"

"Stop the car!" Maggie yelled, finally reacting. She knocked over two bags of groceries, kneeling toward the back to see where Agatha had bolted. The egg cartons were right on top, and the slick, clear goo that had surrounded the yolks began to spread from their containers. Milk was in another bag, but the stiff cardboard corner of one of the egg cartons poked through the thin plastic milk gallon. No one was in a mood for quiche, but there it was in unbaked glory.

I barked as close to the man's ear as I dared, just to make sure he stopped instantly. Maura began to bawl. Who could blame her? The cold, wet snow seeped in the window where the tarp had split when Agatha jumped.

"Now, see here," the driver began, but Annie shushed him.

"You maya broke our car, but you better not oughta broken our Agafa!"

He stopped the jeep. Something in his face said it wasn't the day he had planned either.

I scrambled over the groceries and took off. Agatha sat very still some twenty feet away, quietly nuzzling a strange form sitting on the snow. It was Loretta. I could see as I got closer that she was sound asleep. What was she doing here? She was a good two miles from the boardinghouse.

Maggie was several steps behind me. She had picked the screaming Maura out of her seat and carried her on her hip. Annie was running behind them, and the driver, last out of the jeep, ran so fast he pulled ahead of all of us.

"What the heck . . . ?" He knelt on the ground beside Loretta.

Agatha began to growl. It was a low noise, not truly threatening, but still, a quiet warning.

"It's O.K., girl," the man said, assuring Agatha. "I can help."

I stood beside Agatha, but she hardly noticed me. Her focus was on Loretta. She tenderly nuzzled the woman's hand and cheek.

The driver tried to find Loretta's pulse, while I watched helplessly. It was sad to find Loretta like this. It was sadder to know how much she reminded Agatha of Ardella.

"It's Loretta from the Cavato boardinghouse," Maggie said, walking up with a finally stilled Maura. "I'll go to that green house and call an ambulance."

"Hurry. Her pulse is very slow and she seems awfully cold," the man said. "I'm a paramedic and I've seen cases of hypothermia before."

Annie puffed between Agatha and me. It was a tough run in a down snowsuit.

"Agafa, are you O.K.? Didja hurt your paws or somethin'?" she asked. She didn't even look at Loretta till she was sure Agatha was O.K.

Agatha barked a single firm answer. She was fine. At the sound of that bark, Loretta opened her eyes. She smiled, and we all breathed a sigh of relief.

Chapter 7

When the ambulance arrived, Loretta was sitting up with the young man's leather jacket on her shoulders, Annie's scarf around her neck, Maggie's gloves on her hands, and two Saint Bernards huddled around her in the warming way mastered by our ancestors.

Annie was doing her best to engage Loretta in a profound conversation about "runnin' 'way."

"You shoudn' do that," she said, scolding poor Loretta. "You haffa ask if you wanna walk far."

Loretta seemed to come back from her confused state. She puzzled about her gloves, stroked Agatha and me, and stared at Annie.

"But I didn't mean to go far," she said. "I

needed stamps, and I go to the post office often. . . ."

The danger of the moment seemed to fade as Loretta began to speak.

"My grandson has a birthday. He'll be four. Is that how old you are, young lady?" she asked Annie.

Annie beamed. Four was practically a grownup. She answered like the politician she was becoming. "Well, I almost am. Maybe just almost a year from now, which is nothin'."

Loretta laughed, and we really believed she would be fine. It was a warm, tinkling laugh, and it reassured all of us.

The ambulance had taken seven minutes to get to us. The medics checked Loretta for another five or six minutes before gently putting her aboard. In that time, Annie had already begun to teach her to sing "From Wibbleton to Wobbleton." Loretta clapped her gloved hands. She was quite a sport, and we felt confident that she'd be all right.

Maggie said she'd call the hospital to check on her welfare as soon as we got home. And, of course, Mr. Cavato, and John, Loretta's friend, needed to be told.

I rode home with egg on my tail and milk in

my ear. I figured it would be more chivalrous for me to do that than for Agatha. She angled herself close to the front seat near Maggie. Agatha looked very appreciative, and that made my sacrifice worthwhile. Chivalry will survive the twentieth century at least.

We found Joseph putting his tools in the basket of his three-wheel bike in our driveway. He had found time to fix the sleigh earlier than originally planned, and the coincidence gave us the perfect opportunity to inform him of Loretta's problem. He made a call to the hospital from our house while Maggie unloaded the groceries and helped the driver clean out the back of the jeep. The driver left, finally, and Joseph came in the kitchen for tea.

"Good news?" Maggie asked, setting Maura down to crawl and finding a chocolate chip cookie for Annie.

"Well, it isn't bad," Joseph said, squeezing some lemon in his cup. "They're keeping her for observation overnight. I'll call Loretta's son right away. Did I mention that he's a doctor?"

"For people or animals?" Annie interrupted.

"People. Actually, he specializes in diseases of the aging. He's a gerontologist," Joseph answered. He saw Annie twist her mouth. He couldn't be sure if she was swooshing chocolate from her teeth or about to ask a question. So he explained anyway, "Old people."

"Like Mommy and Daddy?" asked Annie with half a mouthful.

Maggie shot her a glance. "No, dear. Even older than Mom and Dad."

"Why?" Annie used that word more than everyone else in the family put together.

"Well, for one thing, people are living longer, so there's more time for problems to develop," Joseph said.

"Did . . . did she ever have a diagnosis of Alzheimer's disease? A friend—Agatha's former owner . . ." Maggie started to explain about Ardella.

"No, that's not Loretta's problem. There's a family history of epilepsy, and sometimes her medication has to be adjusted. Her son wouldn't have encouraged her to manage on her own if he didn't think she could," Joseph said.

"She ran away for a Pepsi?" It was Annie again.

"No, hon. She has ep-i-lep-sy and her medication made her confused," Maggie said. "She didn't run away. She just got mixed up."

"How cum Agafa saw her before us did?" Annie asked.

"I've been wondering about that myself. I think Agatha has a special instinct . . ." Maggie didn't finish. She walked over to Agatha and gave her a great big hug.

That was a pretty good idea. I was feeling proud of Agatha myself.

". . . a little like Judge has with children," she finished.

I was pleasantly embarrassed. Agatha looked at me, and my temperature went up ten degrees.

Maura, who had been playing with the empty grocery bags on the floor, picked that minute to drape one over my head. I was eternally grateful. I hated being in the limelight: Saint Bernards thrill to a low profile.

George, Joseph's English bulldog who had been sleeping outside in the driveway, pawed at the front door when Seth and Kathleen arrived home from school.

"George, my gosh, I forgot," Joseph stuttered.

Annie let the bulldog in. Joseph was about to grab George and oust him from the house when Maura gurgled, "Gog. Gog, gog, gog."

Everyone turned to stare quietly. It was the first time she had ever said that. In a house with two biggies like Agatha and me. . . .

"Gog." Maura waddled over to George and hugged him. George obliged with his best trick. He rolled over and went to sleep.

Chapter 8

By Friday morning, some good news and some bad surfaced.

Loretta was fine. No hypothermia, just mild exposure. Her son, Dr. Genovese, planned to pick her up at the hospital to spend Christmas at his home in St. Louis. He made arrangements for her to have a medical evaluation at Barnes Hospital, where he was a resident. He brought his Mercedes in to Decatur to his favorite mechanic for its annual once-over, and purchased train tickets for himself and his mother to return to St. Louis. Loretta had been a train buff since she was a child, and her enthusiasm was delightful. With luck, she would be back at the boardinghouse shortly after the first of the year.

The snow ended with not so much as a ground cover. When Joseph Cavato had biked home from our house with George wrapped in one of Annie's old slickers, the fat flakes had poured out of the sky, but they'd melted by the following day, just a wet whimper of a storm.

Tom's business trip flourished. He called with news of two new contracts.

Seth and Kathleen both landed major roles in the Christmas pageant. Annie's entry in the preschool Christmas poster contest was to be featured at the pageant display. She had used Agatha and me as models for a mule and a cow in her manger scene. We must have been sufficient inspiration.

Maura showed positive signs of considering potty training. It was just a nudge in the long haul, but she had begun sitting on the potty chair several times a day with a deck of cards. No one admitted who gave her that idea.

Then the bad chips started rolling in. Maggie heard from Joseph Cavato that Loretta's suitor had become severely depressed during Loretta's absence. With only a week left before Christmas, the morale at the boardinghouse was truly low. No one had even bothered to put the tree up, a job that had been his for years.

A new snowstorm was on its way. This one was backed by two threatening fronts and unlikely to melt in a day like the last flakes. People were warned to stock up and to hole up because it was supposed to be a doozie.

We were still doing our best to think cheerfully, until the snowstorm and Tom tried to come to Decatur together.

Tom called from the airport nine times. First one flight was canceled, then another. It was something that the family had come to expect now and then, but on this particular Friday night, the night of the Christmas pageant, it was a near disaster—especially for Annie. The high point of the program was supposed to include a certain father decked out in a Santa suit.

The bright red velvet suit, the shiny black belt, the beard, the hat were carefully laid out on the bed. But the body who had happily volunteered to do the honors was stuck in an airport several hundred miles away. Poor Tom.

Maggie dished up Sloppy Joes to a roomful of sulking faces.

"Annie, you know if there were any way . . ." Maggie didn't finish. She looked at Annie's watery eyes and knew it was no use.

"How will we get there, Mom?" Kathleen asked.

"We can call friends for a ride. I'm sure we can find someone. Or if that doesn't work, we'll just splurge for a cab," Maggie answered.

"And the Santa suit?" Seth asked.

"We'll call someone about that, too," Maggie said. "There will be lots of fathers going, and they'll be glad to do it. We'll just bring the outfit and go a little early."

Tears began to pour down Annie's face. "But it isna gonna be the same."

"No, honey. It won't be the same." Maggie put extra potato chips on Annie's plate, but Annie just looked at them. She wasn't eating a thing.

Seth tried to cheer her up. "Boy, if this snow keeps up, we're going to have a great time building snow forts this weekend, huh, Annie?"

"And snow angels," Kathleen said. "Nobody does those better than you, Annie."

It seemed as if all the Christmas brightness had been zapped out of Annie. Suddenly, the Christmas brightness seemed zapped out of the whole house.

We heard a long, loud crack—and then we sat in total darkness. Every light, every clock, everything electrical flashed out.

There was a silent pause, then Maggie said, "Just give it a minute, kids. The electricity always comes right back on."

Kathleen was already fumbling through the kitchen drawers for candles and matches. Seth got the flashlight from its spot over the back door and beamed it on the supper table.

"Go ahead and finish, kids," Maggie told them.

But as I bit into my Sloppy Joe, it didn't taste quite the same. I sat down and looked at Agatha. She wasn't eating either.

We waited and waited. The clink of the dishes was the only sound.

Chapter 9

After ten minutes, Maggie lit several candles and began clearing the table.

"Maybe we better call the power company," Kathleen suggested as she rinsed dishes in the near dark.

"It can't hurt. Sometimes, if it's a local transformer . . . go ahead, Seth, you're closest," Maggie said.

Seth picked up the phone. "That's out, too."

Maggie turned from the sink. "It is?"

"Then how are we going to find a ride?" Kathleen said, putting the last of the silverware in the dishwasher. "Maybe we should have washed these by hand."

"Seth, go stand on the porch and see if the Lockleys or anybody down the road has lights," Maggie said.

He came back quickly. "I've never seen it so dark. Maybe they'll call off the Christmas program. I'll get the radio and see if there are any announcements."

The transistor failed us, too. It played for a few seconds, then the batteries breathed their last.

"Mom?" Kathleen looked at Maggie. She lifted Maura out of her highchair and waited for a miracle from her mother.

"Seth, what about the snow?" Maggie asked.

"It's real pretty," Seth said. He was finishing the last of the brownies.

"Seth!" Maggie's firmness caught him that time.

"Oh, you mean . . . well, it's probably only a couple of inches deep, but it is still coming down. Not real heavy, though. The worst of it is where Dad is—we won't get the heavy stuff till morning. At least that's what the TV said earlier." Seth swept the crumbs into his hand and put them in the garbage. In the dark, most missed.

I cleaned up for him.

Annie had gotten down from the table and

was leaning on Agatha. She didn't seem particularly interested in the discussion. The darkness fit her mood.

Maggie looked around the room.

"What we all need is a little Christmas spirit," she said. "Annie, dear, how would you like to ride to the pageant in a sleigh . . ."

Annie sat up.

". . . pulled not by eight tiny reindeer but by two gorgeous Saint Bernards?"

Gorgeous? Saint Bernards?

Annie cocked her head to one side. "Really?"

"All right!" Seth shouted.

"Let's pull it out of the garage before we get our costumes on." Kathleen had already grabbed me by the collar and was reaching for Agatha. When Seth hesitated, Kathleen gave him a hard nudge. "Now, brother. Before Mom changes her mind. It's going to be slower than a car, so we'd better get a move on."

Mayhem erupted. Everyone moved at breakneck speed getting everyone else hopping at once.

I never knew Maura and Annie could get ready so fast. Seth looked strange with a blue parka over his shepherd costume, especially when Maggie insisted he wear earmuffs, too.

Annie was beginning to bounce back. She couldn't hide her smile.

Every flashlight we could find was securely tied to the front and back of the sleigh. When Maggie worried that there still wouldn't be enough light, Seth found a box of Fourth of July firework sparklers and some matches. He said he'd ride in the back and play taillight.

Kathleen carried her angel wings.

Agatha and I were hitched to the sleigh with leather harnesses and jingle bells. The mood was instant-merry. We were just about ready to take off when Maggie remembered the Santa suit.

She went back in the house, stopping once to wink at me. "What do you say, Judge—if the 'suit' fits . . . ?" she whispered.

When our driver came back out to the sleigh several minutes later, it wasn't Maggie at all. It was a strange figure wearing an oversized red velvet suit, a white beard, and a patent leather belt that held pillows in place. "It" stomped toward us in huge black boots, stuffed with newspaper to keep from falling off Maggie's size-five feet.

Annie giggled, a little bit at first, but was soon laughing a full-fledged laugh.

"Oh, Mommy!"

Maggie responded with a high-pitched "Ho, ho, ho!"

The pillows slipped, showing ruffled chintz under the red velvet.

By the time Maggie had positioned herself in the front seat of the sleigh, she had exchanged the pillows for Maura and buckled her in place.

"On Comet, on Cupid!" Maggie yelled between ho-hos.

Seth put his hands on his Mom's shoulder. "I think a simple 'giddyap' will do it."

Kathleen was laughing so hard little tears formed in the corners of her eyes. The loudest noise came from Maura, screaming at the top of her lungs as Agatha and I trotted out of the driveway and down the road.

The best I could make out, it was a twelve-syllable "*Wheeeeeeeeeeeeeeee!*"

The ride was incredible. We pulled up safely at the school to unload, each of us buoyed by the experience. Instead of darkness, we were greeted with a serendipitous surge of electricity. The lights went back on. Decatur's and ours.

Chapter 10

The maiden voyage of the O'Riley-Hoffman sleigh had been nothing short of perfect. Agatha's strength amazed me. I had expected to do twice the pulling since she was still pounds lighter than me, but it was actually she who set the trotting pace.

She looked beautiful as she held her head high. We didn't even feel cold, but then Saint Bernards are bred for that. I was proud to be part of this team.

Seth doused the last of the fireworks in the snow when Father Sestak greeted us at the main sidewalk. Father was flanked by two gentlemen with large flashlights—the kind with the long cylindrical red end like theater ushers use. They had been steering people into parking spaces because the parking lot lights had been out.

"Maggie? Uh . . ." Father Sestak seemed at a genuine loss for words.

Maggie got down and hoisted her pants for the umpteenth time. She handed Maura to Mr. Zindel and replaced the pillows. Maura proceeded to teethe on the red flashlight.

"Good evening, Father. Are we a bit early?" Maggie asked.

Mr. Cavanaugh waved the other flashlight and laughed. "Tom chickened out, eh?"

Annie rescued Mr. Zindel's flashlight from Maura. He had been too busy staring at the disheveled Santa to realize that Maura could inflict permanent injury to herself and the beam.

Between Annie and Mr. Cavanaugh, the arcs of light passed back and forth over the sidewalk like searchlights. It didn't take long for a crowd to gather.

"Are them Clydesdales, Hal?" We heard one voice from near the evergreens.

"Nope, Dottie. Them's huskies. Everybody knows that!" The answer was indignant.

Agatha and I looked at each other. For a brief moment—with the lights and the attention—I had been feeling a little like a movie star at a premiere. What was that saying? Pride goeth before a fall?

We were prepared to wait under the carport during the program, but Father Sestak would have none of that. We were unhitched and escorted to the room where the shepherds and cast were putting on their makeup. Sister Mary Clare used muslin sheeting to dry the snow from our backs and paws. Even though we wouldn't be able to see the program itself, we would be able to hear it. We settled in against the bingo tables in the backstage makeup room.

Cass Dawson and Billy Passerelli had to stand with their noses against the blackboard when Sister Melanie caught them dueling with their shepherd's canes as swords. That lasted as long as it took them to discover the erasers. Round two began in a cloud of chalk. Sister Mary Clare finally put them to work making new braces for a scenery flat that kept teetering and threatening to collapse.

Katy MacVey's angel wings got caught in a slamming door and had to be rebuilt.

Mrs. Swanson, the head makeup lady, got a little carried away and managed to smear a bright red #2 lipstick stripe on Saint Joseph. It was only a matter of time till Annie discovered the tube and tried her hand at making Agatha a painted lady.

Oh, boy. Lucky for Agatha, Kathleen came in time to avert a messy disaster.

Somehow, the elements of the pageant came together just five minutes later than the predicted curtain time.

The music of the children's voices was enough to put anyone in a Christmas mood. By the last scene, when Kathleen as Angel Gabriel–Narrator asked the audience to join in singing "Silent Night," Agatha and I were moved enough to add our own melodic howls.

It wasn't high opera, but it was sincere.

None of us wanted to see the evening end. When the family piled into the sleigh for the ride home, Maggie came up with an ideal suggestion. Since Loretta's friend at the boardinghouse had not been in the mood to put up the Christmas tree, maybe we could go by and do it for him. A little cheer could go a long way and we were all in the mood to help.

We took our time on the ride, enjoying the Christmas lights that had not been on before in the homes along the way. We were busy admiring the decorations, and were hardly prepared for another kind of light in the boardinghouse driveway. We counted three flashing red sirens and saw a half-dozen police on Joseph Cavato's porch.

I hoped the police weren't going to ask me for a chauffeur's license. Or Maggie for some kind of sticker. Or arrest Agatha and me for improper leashing . . . or hauling . . . or . . .

"Maggie, I've been trying to call you." Joseph ran out on the porch as soon as he saw us. "Loretta's gone again."

Agatha's back stiffened and her face froze in fear.

Maggie got out of the sleigh. She was still wearing the Santa suit, minus the beard.

Joseph stepped back. "Boy, you really got in the spirit of it, didn't you?"

The kids piled out to go into the house to warm up. "Where's George?" Annie asked, looking around.

"George is missing, too," Joseph said. "But the one has nothing to do with the other. Loretta was in her hospital room while her son, Dr. Genovese, was downstairs signing the release forms to take her home. She was all set to go, standing with an orderly, waiting for the elevator—then the electricity blacked out."

"Maybe she's still somewhere in the hospital," Maggie said hopefully.

"They've searched and searched. The orderly sat her down in a chair by the nurse's station and left for a second to help someone else during the blackout," Joseph explained. "He had no idea leaving Loretta would cause a problem. Believe me, even without everyone's help, he has covered that hospital a dozen times."

"But hadn't her medication been adjusted?" Maggie asked.

"That's the worst part. Dr. Genovese had her medicine. He was taking charge of adjusting her dosage—he wanted to monitor it himself. It was just the most incredibly bad timing."

"Doesn't the hospital have auxiliary generators?" Maggie wanted to know.

"It takes several minutes to activate them, and that was time enough for her to disappear," Joseph explained.

"And George?" Maggie asked.

I saw Agatha's ears perk up.

"Not a clue. Dad doesn't even remember letting him out, but he must have. I was at the hospital with Dr. Genovese. We came back here on the chance someone had found her and brought her home." Joseph looked at Agatha and me. "I was hoping for another one of your Saint Bernard miracles." He shook his head sadly.

Maggie looked at the snow and shook her head, too.

We heard a bit of commotion coming from inside the house. Annie and Maura could get into a lot of trouble without George to entertain them.

"I'd better get my crew home," Maggie said. Decorating a Christmas tree was out of the question now. "The little ones can't exactly help."

I couldn't help thinking about the coincidence of both George and Loretta disappearing on the same night. It was a bit too bizarre. How far away was the hospital? Could George have known Loretta was nearby and in trouble? Could Loretta have headed for the boarding-house? Or what?

"If Tom gets back, he can bring the Saints to help you look," Maggie offered.

"I'll call you, Maggie. That is, *if* the phones stay working. They've been going on and off, too," Joseph said.

Maggie nodded, knowing about the phones firsthand. "Maybe we'll get lucky again. Someone may bring Loretta back soon."

Somehow the rest of the ride seemed cold.

Agatha tensed with each step. The news at the boardinghouse had really upset her. Snowflakes that had tasted fresh and bright before seemed heavy and wet now.

Annie began fussing with Maura. Seth jumped out to open the garage door, and Maggie carefully turned the sleigh around so we could push it in backward.

Kathleen unhooked Agatha's harness first. That's when we heard Annie yell.

"George?"

Sure enough, there was George, huffing and puffing down our road. He stopped to pant and stared hard at Agatha. Then he turned around and started running.

Agatha didn't hesitate but went charging down the road after him, dragging her unfastened harness.

"Agafa, you cum back here!" Annie was shaking her finger and screaming.

I barked and barked. *Someone* get me out of this harness!

Seth and Kathleen were running down the road, trying to stop Agatha instead of unleashing me.

I barked louder. Wait for me, Agatha, please! Agatha was nearly out of sight.

Please!

I howled, the noisiest, most blood-curdling howl I could muster.

Maggie unhooked me. "Judge, we don't want to lose you both." But she knew I had to go.

Maggie stepped aside. I took in all the air my lungs could stand and charged after Agatha and George.

Chapter 11

The snow stopped. The still, cold night wrapped around me, making me shiver. Which way had Agatha gone?

I wasn't much for tracking, and footprints on a snowy road are hard to see. I barked. Surely Agatha would answer me . . . but I heard nothing.

I turned in circles, trying to figure out just where to go, and found a single bell caught in a shrub at the road's fork. It could have come from the harness. I took off in that direction and thought I saw a small figure yards ahead. Too small for Agatha.

George?

He could not keep up a marathon for long. This was a dog who believed his body was designed for holding up his head. No matter how good his motives were, he would fade.

Gradually, I saw the figure getting closer. I got faster and he got slower. He kept stopping to rest, panting hard.

At least I knew I was going the right way.

We were nearly even when I saw the railroad tracks. I didn't realize we had run so far. The Amtrak station was crowded with Christmastime travelers.

That's when I saw Agatha. I was yards behind her, and she was close to the tracks and trains. I didn't like it.

Then I spotted Loretta. She was just ahead of Agatha and paying little attention to the dangers around her—moving trains, rushing crowds, the tracks. . . .

Loretta was walking parallel to a track loading passengers on the Panama Limited. She was close to the edge of the track, and her pace was less than steady.

Agatha caught up with Loretta, stepping carefully in front of her. If she could stop her, get her attention . . . but Loretta looked annoyed and kept moving.

Trains on two tracks were starting. The clank of wheels grinded a warning.

Dear Agatha. Please be careful.

Agatha tried again. Why didn't anyone else notice this woman? There were people all around. Loretta was dazed, confused. Had she taken more medicine from the nurse's station before leaving the hospital? Were people so caught up in their own Christmas plans that they didn't care?

I was getting close enough to see Agatha's face, her deep brown eyes and thick eyebrows folded in worry.

Finally, Loretta stopped. She looked at Agatha and slumped her shoulders, acting suddenly very tired. Then she did the terrible thing none of us could have predicted or could have stopped.

Loretta looked at the crowds of people boarding the Panama and turned away to another train, a supply train, with tankers and flatbeds and freezer cabs. She stepped on an empty flatbed nearby and lay down.

I heard the clanking and grinding of wheels again. No. It couldn't be . . . but it was.

Loretta was asleep or had blacked out or something—and the flatbed where she lay was

rolling into motion, chugging slowly down the track.

I was still yards away when Agatha saw me. She kept looking at Loretta and then at me. The train picked up speed.

No Agatha, please . . .

But I saw Agatha's look. I was sure she was remembering that the last time her first mistress had left, she had never seen her again.

Agatha jumped on the flatbed beside Loretta. The train went faster. I could not go fast enough.

I barked, I jumped, but it was too late. I watched Agatha go, and fear and anger began to fill me up.

That's when I felt a strong hand on my collar.

Chapter 12

"Judge? What on earth are you doing here?" The strong hand belonged to Tom. Frustrated with the repeated delays at the airport, he had wangled his way on an Amtrak.

If only he had walked up minutes earlier! Now how was I going to explain?

I ran up and down the track, barking, but he didn't understand. Then dear George came huffing and puffing our way.

Tom knew George from his morning jog, and though Tom could not really know what was going on, he put two and two together well enough to know where to go to find out.

"George? We better get you home." Tom

stooped to his knees to pet the panting bulldog. George, in exasperation and in character, put his chin to Tom's thigh and fell asleep.

Tom picked up two suitcases in one hand and balanced George under his other arm. "Phones haven't been working. We'll have to pay for our ride home. C'mon, Judge."

We trekked through the station, an unlikely travel group, but no one seemed to notice. Except the cab driver.

"No pets." He spat the words out without dislodging his cigar.

"Well, sir, this is something of an emergency," Tom began politely.

George let out a good snore.

The cab driver just grunted again, "No pets."

I admired Tom's politeness, but it wasn't working.

I walked up close to the driver, who had turned the other way, and in his left ear I gave him my biggest woof.

He dropped the cigar.

"Well, O.K., maybe this one time . . ."

Bingo.

Tom opened the back cab door and jumped in before my scare wore off.

We went to the boardinghouse first to deliver

George. Joseph thanked Tom for bringing George home and filled Tom in on the evening. But there were still pieces to be put together. Tom hurried home to talk to Maggie.

The cab driver charged us for three fares. I was so tired and discouraged, I didn't even feel like trying to woof him out of it.

Maggie and the kids spent precious time hugging Tom—and all I could do was sit and wait.

When Maggie and Tom finally finished telling each other what they knew, the phones were working again. It took two agonizing hours to fill in the gaps and get to the bottom of Loretta's story.

Dr. Genovese had learned from Joseph that Loretta still had some of her old medication in her purse and may have taken some herself. No one at the hospital would have noticed because she kept it in her rosary case rather than in a pillbox. Several train magazines on her nightstand had parts of advertisements torn out that featured train discounts for senior citizens. Dr. Genovese nearly cried when he realized that his plan for Loretta's Christmas trip home on a train may have pushed her, in her confused state, to find the trains herself. But Dr. Baker provided the critical clue. He had been at the station picking up his own holiday tickets and noticed a strange lady—he thought she was a roving bag lady—by the supply train where he also went to check on medical freight. What aroused his curiosity was that he noticed a Saint Bernard with her and had been calling Saint Bernard owners to see if anyone's dog was missing. When he made the call to Tom, he learned that George and I had both been there.

Everything began to fit. Dr. Baker said what I could not. The sheriff took his investigation to the Amtrak station. Dr. Genovese was worried about Loretta's confused state of mind but convinced himself and us that if she spent time in a clinic, her medication could be monitored and adjusted to the correct dosage. The aging process changes the body's chemistry, and drug reactions late in life are often hard to determine. Loretta might have taken just an ordinary dosage and found it too strong.

We had to find her—and Agatha.

We waited by the phone, all of us crowded around the kitchen table, never mind that bedtime was long gone. Maggie didn't even put Maura down. Instead, she let her fidget quietly in the playpen with a brooding Annie.

Maggie offered everyone hot chocolate, cookies, and a game of Life, but no one wanted anything.

Just word, word that Agatha was all right and Loretta . . .

It came at eleven-thirty.

Maggie picked up the phone before the end of the first ring. Silence. Maggie sighed deeply. She covered the phone with her hand.

"They're O.K.—both of them! The police found them in Peoria after the all-points bulletin went out." Maggie was breathless telling the news. "They were sitting in the square by the Civic Center. Agatha stayed with Loretta. No one knows why or when they left the train. I guess Agatha kept barking and pestering some people until they called the police, and they knew about the bulletin."

Agatha did it. She pulled it off. She had protected her new friend!

As soon as Maggie hung up the phone, she picked it up again to dial Dr. Baker. Late or not, he had asked to be kept informed, and she decided to persuade him to come over and take a look at Agatha. Missing that appointment had been one thing, but Maggie wanted to be sure Agatha was O.K. after tonight's ordeal.

Agatha was escorted home by Sheriff Fischer.

He kept patting her and talking proudly. He had always been a dog lover, and Agatha had proved herself a real heroine.

But I noticed that Agatha walked up the outside stairs to the house very slowly. She appeared tired and weak.

Sheriff Fischer tried to help her along. A lump filled my throat.

"Agafa?" Annie said. Even her little voice carried a squeak of hesitation.

Agatha stepped through the front door. She went to Annie and gave her a Saint Bernard kiss. She turned to little Maura and nudged her hand. Then she stepped toward me . . .

. . . and collapsed.

Kathleen screeched, "Agatha!"

Seth was already kneeling beside her.

I was frozen to my spot. What could I do? What was happening? Agatha? Had we found her only to lose her again?

"Dad, what happened? Is she hurt?" Kathleen was stroking Agatha's forehead.

"I wish Agatha could talk," Tom said. "I'd like to hear her story."

I had somehow moved my stiff body toward Agatha, close enough to hear she was still breathing evenly.

Maggie came in with a wet cloth for Agatha's head. Sheriff Fischer had gone to his car for his first-aid kit, though what he had that Maggie's medicine cabinet didn't was beyond me. Seth went to get a pillow but didn't quite know what to do with it since both Kathleen and I were blocking his way. He just stood there, hugging it to his chest.

Maggie reached for the pillow and raised Agatha's head. She touched a cool towel to Agatha's eyes, her nose, her neck.

No one even noticed Dr. Baker's knock, if he did knock. We just saw him stride in the front door carrying a racquetball racquet in one hand and a black bag in the other. Racquetball? At midnight? But it wasn't the time to ask questions.

Tom looked up. "Dr. Baker, thanks for coming so late," he said. He tried to shake Dr. Baker's hand, but the bag and the racquet got in the way.

Dr. Baker knelt down, and Maggie shooed everyone out of his way. I kept scooting up for a better look until Dr. Baker and I were eyeball to eyeball.

"Now, Judge," he said, "do you think you're helping?"

I crawled back.

Tom spoke in broken sentences. "We don't think . . . I mean, she's been gone for hours . . . but there were no signs of an accident. . . ."

Dr. Baker examined Agatha very carefully. He took his time, slowly going over every inch of her. He whispered soothingly as he went along.

Agatha opened her eyes.

"You have a surprise for everyone, don't you, girl?" Dr. Baker said finally. He was not frowning. He didn't even look worried. He broke into a great big smile.

"Did a bit too much for a mother-to-be, didn't you?" Dr. Baker grinned.

It took a few seconds to soak in. Seth looked at Kathleen. Maggie looked at Tom. I kept looking at Agatha. We looked at each other. I looked at the ceiling, the floor, the nearby doorknob. Then Annie gave a jump and grabbed little Maura in a fireman's clinch.

"Puppies!"

As if on cue, Agatha slowly sat up.

She looked tired and weak, but a beam of light seemed to glow from behind those big brown eyes.

Puppies. Our puppies. If Agatha was going to

be a mother, that meant another important thing. . . . I was going to be a father.

It hit me like a lightning bolt.

That's when I fainted.

Chapter 13

Dr. Baker called before noon the next day to confirm his test results. Agatha Bliss was indeed going to have puppies. I couldn't even eat. Maggie accused me of faking morning sickness. Everybody laughed when she said that, except me. I really didn't feel well.

There's always a period of adjustment, I suppose.

But not for Agatha. After twenty-four hours of good rest, she was a new woman. Rejuvenated. Full of energy. She even gave up her late-morning snooze and took long walks around the yard. It drove me crazy.

For my sake as well as Agatha's, Tom began

taking her on his morning jog. She'd stop at the halfway point, Joseph's boardinghouse, visit with George and the boarders, and have a bowl of milk, then jog home with Tom on his return run. It would be really nice when Loretta got back. Agatha could spend that special time with Loretta.

I began sleeping in. I'd dream a lot about things like many little pups climbing all over me and asking me questions—or one jumping in the pool, and me not getting there fast enough. . . . I'd wake in a cold shake.

How was I going to get through this?

Annie brought me puppy pictures daily. "See, Judge?" she'd say, laying out the magazine spots she had expertly removed from Maggie's periodicals. "We're gonna hab cute kids. I just know it."

She showed me a lot of beagles. And poodles. It occurred to me that she might be very disappointed. Would ours suffer by comparison?

One day, Maura decided to study Annie's picture collection. When Annie wasn't looking, she picked them up one by one and took them in the kitchen. In one of those dreadful moments of good intentions, Maura dropped them into a sink full of soapy water to clean them.

Annie was furious. She not only threatened Maura with bodily harm, but threatened to squeal to Santa Claus about her sister's bad behavior. It was a good thing Maura was too young to understand.

When Maggie discovered the mess in the kitchen, she was pretty furious, too. Annie and I both got a lecture on the dangers of Maura playing in water.

She was right, of course. I had been so wrapped up in my own fantasies, I'd neglected to do my job. After that, I paid more attention to the children. That made the days go faster.

On Christmas Eve, shortly after the special five o'clock children's Mass, Dr. Baker stopped by. He was in time for the hot chocolate and homemade candy that Maggie had prepared to encourage an early bedtime for the kids.

Dr. Baker had begun to grow a beard. When pecan crumbles from the pralines he was eating disappeared in his beard, he seemed puzzled as to how to politely remove them. Everyone wondered how to help. Maura didn't wonder at all. She climbed on his lap, put a hand to his chin, and tugged the little sugary nuts out of their grizzly hiding. Then she ate them.

Poor Dr. Baker. Thank goodness he likes kids.

"Well, you just have a few more weeks of peace and quiet." He laughed, watching Maura.

I hardly would have described any days in the O'Riley house as peaceful and quiet, but we knew what he meant.

Maura got down from his lap when she noticed the marshmallows floating in his hot chocolate cup. They were within toddler reach on the end table, and she began to rescue them from the same fate as the pralines in Dr. Baker's beard.

Maggie noticed but looked away. I think this was one of those gray areas of motherhood.

"Still snowing?" Tom asked, getting up to pass the candy.

"A little. Not enough to spoil our trip," Dr. Baker answered. He reached for Maggie's homemade caramels. They looked as if they would enter his mouth in one piece and stay there.

"Nice of you to pay us a visit before you leave. Christmas in Sannibel Island again?" Maggie had disappeared momentarily into the kitchen to grab a paper towel. She quietly attended to the dripping fist of Maura, who was now putting some marshmallow rejects *back* into Dr. Baker's hot chocolate.

"We won't leave till the day after," Dr. Baker

answered, nodding. "I'm like you. I like Christmas morning at home with the kids. Taking the train this time is going to be a real kick."

"You comin' back for Agafa's big day, right?" Annie asked.

"That's the plan," he said. "But I've brought a few things over now to help you get ready."

Dr. Baker handed a large brown envelope to Seth who was sitting closest. Seth couldn't say anything, though, because his mouth was full of caramels *and* pralines.

So Kathleen spoke. "Get ready?"

"You'll want to prepare a birthing box," he explained. "There are some simple directions in the envelope. And there are things to watch for to make sure Agatha is getting along O.K. It will also tell you when to call me."

"You're not expecting any special problems, are you?" Maggie asked. "I mean, the infection years ago . . ."

"Nope. We're expecting fine pups. Maybe not a large litter, but fine pups." He got up off the couch and walked to the area near the Christmas tree where Agatha and I were lying. He patted us both and studied Agatha carefully.

"Maggie, Tom, these are really special dogs in a special breed. I've watched Judge gentle your little ones through childhood, and now these stories of Agatha with Ardella and Loretta . . ." He paused.

Everyone, even Annie and Maura, sat quietly for a moment, looking at Agatha and me.

I had the most peculiar sensation, as if someone was reaching into my heart and making me feel better. Agatha's paw scooted closer to mine.

Dr. Baker headed toward the front door. "Best I be getting home," he said finally. "My trunk is full of presents that need to be wrapped. I put a few interesting articles in that envelope you might want to read. They're studying many possibilities of dogs helping not just the blind, but also people with other handicaps."

"I've heard something about that," Maggie said thoughtfully, getting his coat from the hall closet. She was looking at us and not at Dr. Baker when she said it.

By the time Dr. Baker's car pulled out of the drive, Tom was already steering the kids to bed. Maggie walked into the empty living room, her hands in her pockets and her face thoughtful. Finally she spoke to us. "You know what, guys? The beauty and brains of the Saint Bernard have been overlooked and underappreciated."

Tom came back in in time for the last three

words. "Overlooked and underappreciated? I certainly am!"

Maggie laughed and gave him a hug.

"Kids asleep?" she asked.

"Close," he answered.

"Then we better get busy."

Agatha and I were allowed to share the secrets of that Christmas Eve. We watched Maggie and Tom wrap and assemble, fuss and laugh. We heard them talk about other Christmases and other presents. When all was ready, we saw them share one quiet early gift together.

Tom put a ring on Maggie's finger. It had four simple stones arranged like flowers in a garden, each a birthstone for one of the children.

Maggie pulled a small box from behind the manger and handed it to Tom. It was a plain crystal paperweight with these words: *The reward for love is the capacity for more love.*

They sat quietly after that, as did Agatha and I. Nothing in a box could be richer than the gift we already shared.

Chapter 14

The weeks after Christmas brought a lot of wet weather—some snow, some ice, some cold rain.

Little could be done on Tom's construction sites, so he spent a lot of time "putzing," as Maggie called it, around the house. In spite of the weather, he roughed out a shed for storing the sled. He made it large enough for other things as well, joking about overflowing Saint Bernards.

I hoped he was talking about numbers and not pounds.

Then he got busy on the birthing box.

Seth and Kathleen woke early on a sleep-in Saturday to help.

"Seth, you can't hammer with sticky hands," Kathleen scolded. "You're getting doughnut glaze all over the handle."

Seth finished his doughnut in one bite and wiped his hands on his jeans. Then he wiped the hammer handle on his shirt. Kathleen groaned.

"Who cut this board?" Tom interrupted. "It's two inches too short, and it's my last long piece."

Seth and Kathleen looked at each other. Neither would turn the other guy in.

Tom looked around the garage for something else. If he wanted to finish the box in one morning, he'd have to settle for his supplies on hand. He spotted a large piece of plexiglass leaning against the wall, and fired up the heater to bend the clear plastic.

Seth and Kathleen finished nailing together the three sides of measured wood. Then Tom "folded" the warm plexiglass between the wooden slats to serve as the fourth side.

Kathleen went to the back door and got Agatha's rug. She smoothed it in the bottom of the new box.

"Agatha!" Seth didn't have to call her more than once. Agatha had spent the last few days digging into the rug and scratching at her own spot on the floor, and she immediately understood. The O'Rileys had made a nest for her puppies.

She jumped inside the box, sniffing carefully and nodding her approval. But when Annie, Maura, and I moved closer to have a better look, she told us in no uncertain woofs that the box was reserved. At her request, she and I slept apart. I knew the time for giving birth was near.

Tom put an electric heater in the garage to keep the temperature warmer than normal. It was too hot for me, but Dr. Baker's instructions had been explicit. Every so often, I would wander into the garage and check through the plexiglass side—Tom's makeshift design had made it easy for me. Then I would leave Agatha to her fitful napping.

Maggie went in regularly, too, taking Agatha's temperature and monitoring other telltale signs.

On Sunday morning, I heard her call Dr. Baker. Then she announced to the family, "He's on his way. Giving birth takes a while, so we're all going to church as usual."

Church?

Seth pleaded, Kathleen faked tears, Annie cried real tears, but Maggie was adamant. Nothing short of plague or earthquake would keep the family from Sunday Mass.

But leave me? At a time like this? I tried to sit down. It lasted three seconds. I stood up. Then I waltzed around in a circle. I barked at everybody who ran bathwater and nudged everyone coming and going down the hall.

They couldn't really leave!

"Judge Benjamin, please!" Maggie tried to calm me down. "Nothing's going to happen for a while, and Dr. Baker will be here in five minutes. The rest of us would probably be in the way."

Dr. Baker arrived in two minutes.

"Ho," he said, waving. "How are we doing?"

Maggie answered, "Mom is coming along fine, but expectant father is something of a nervous wreck." She pointed to me. I couldn't argue with that.

"Well, go on off to Mass and we'll keep things under control," he said. "I just delivered six kittens at the Masons, and I'm expecting a red litter day." He laughed at his own joke and headed for Agatha.

I watched the family pull out of the driveway, Annie still arguing about a window seat and Maura chewing on Seth's scarf. Then I followed Dr. Baker.

Agatha didn't seem to object to the doctor's

presence, but she was less than thrilled with mine. I made her nervous. My anxiety was contagious, and my pounding heart echoed through the garage.

"Judge," Dr. Baker said firmly, "this won't do. You have to leave."

I couldn't. I just couldn't.

Maybe I could try the old "out of sight, out of mind" routine. A stack of paint cans were lined up on the front of the radial saw bench near Dr. Baker. I backed in behind that, trying not to breathe. Agatha seemed to calm down with me out of sight, and Dr. Baker said no more.

I couldn't hear anything, and not only could Agatha not see me, but I couldn't see her. I sat on my hind legs, peeking around the paint cans. In the clumsiest gesture of my entire life, I accidentally knocked a can of seafoam green off the top of the stack!

I don't think Dr. Baker had any idea what hit him. One minute he was listening to Agatha's heart through his stethoscope, and the next minute he was out cold on the floor of the garage.

What had I done? Agatha was about to give birth to our puppies and I'd all but killed the doctor!

What could I do? If I went to the neighbors',

they'd never understand. It would be an hour before the family returned, and somebody needed to be with Agatha.

There was only one place to go for guidance at a time like this. I opened the back door, jumped the fence, and raced to church. The O'Rileys would understand.

I knew I'd never get past the ushers, so I headed for the sacristy door at the back of the altar. That meant there was only one way to get to the O'Rileys once I was inside, and that was past the priest.

There I was, trying to tip-paw across the altar, searching the congregation for the O'Rileys, and there Father Sestak was, trying to finish his homily. He cleared his throat and ended his sermon with, "All creatures great and small . . . the Lord God loves them all."

Then he led me to my family.

Chapter 15

Seafoam green would probably be the color of the garage floor forever, but it didn't matter. By the time we got back to the house, Dr. Baker was sitting on the workbench holding an ice pack to the back of his head and pointing to the birthing box with the other.

It was full of small, squirming creatures and one calm, great one—Agatha.

"Mom, they look like wet socks," Annie said.

Wet socks? My kids? Annie!

I looked carefully. Their eyes were not open yet. Their little round heads folded into their bodies without any noticeable necks. Their fur was damp from birth. Their paws coiled inward like firm fuzzballs.

If I had found them under the bed, I probably would have thought the same thing as Annie.

"When I woke up, Mom and pups were doing fine," Dr. Baker said, smiling. He didn't seem a bit bothered that his khaki pants and V-neck sweater now matched the floor. "She didn't need any of us to pull this off. And she did it in record time, too."

Dr. Baker turned to me. My guilt was a heavy burden, but his face was kind. There was no scold in his voice.

Agatha looked up from the pups. Dr. Baker and Maggie had both warned me for days that she would not put up with much of me just after the pups were born. But I guess Agatha had other instincts, too. Maybe she sensed my pain. She stood up carefully and, with her mouth, lifted the closest pup toward me. The legs unfolded into useful limbs and the chin separated from the chest, showing a finely shaped body.

It was a boy, and I knew from the look in Agatha's eyes that it was our firstborn. He had dark, rich puppy fur, still wet and wavy behind the ears. His yawn was peaceful. Except for a Swiss ear, the hospice mark that spotted the ear

as if it had been dipped in snow, he looked exactly like my own puppy pictures.

I felt funny—proud, but very funny.

One by one, Agatha lifted each of the pups. She'd had a small litter, just as Dr. Baker had predicted. Three boys and one girl.

"'Bout time we evened the score," Tom said, patting me on the head.

Everyone was watching the puppies. Annie had to be restrained from jumping in and grabbing one. Kathleen had gotten the camera and was taking pictures. No one noticed Maura bending over the birthing box until two feet dangled toward the ceiling as she stood on her head—*inside.*

Even on special days, some things are business as usual.

I reached in, grabbed the seat of her pants, and right-sided her.

Chapter 16

The sheen of the wet sock look soon became the thick fluff of puppy fur. It was so soft. I liked nothing better than to have the pups climb on my paws so I could feel their rich, cottony fur. Maggie said the fur would change in a matter of weeks, so I wanted every chance to touch it.

In ten days, when the puppies' eyes opened and the room didn't have to be quite so warm, Maggie moved the birthing box into the kitchen. We didn't want to miss a minute. On the twelfth day, their ears opened. Maggie had to clean them carefully with mineral oil, and then it was time to clip and sand their nails. Finally, the puppies could be held, and Annie and Maura spent the entire day begging for turns.

After getting to know the pups, we named them. We had found out a lot about those pups in just a few weeks, and by the time they stood at a wobbly two weeks old, we watched them grow into their names.

The firstborn became Chancellor McKenna—Chancey for short. He regularly risked life and limb as Maura's sidekick. Twice I pulled him from the fireplace ashes as he was leading Maura into the soot. When Maura took a bath, Chancey appeared out of nowhere and fell in. His favorite sport was to dive-bomb into the diaper pail, both he and Maura flinging the diapers to parts unknown. Once, we discovered Chancey in Maura's playpen *under* her receiving blanket, next to sleeping Maura. We might have spent hours looking for him except that he was so happy that he wagged his tail back and forth under the blanket, like a flag of surrender. He couldn't help being proud of his trick, squeezing through the wooden slats and finding her.

We called the second pup Sir Abercrombie—Annie called him ABC Crummy, but he didn't seem to mind. Sir Abercrombie considered himself a lapdog, and anybody's lap would do. His paws were big, really big, and his thick neck grew thicker daily. He had the only half mask in the litter, and it made him look like a football fullback with one remarkable shiner.

When Kathleen undertook a photojournalism project in conjunction with the Science and Arts Fair, Abercrombie became her willing subject. His cooperation knew no bounds. Given the dedication of those two, and the zillions of flashing bulbs that went off daily, the whole family expected a blue-ribbon finish.

Doc Jory, marked with the monk's cap, was third in line and our thinker. The first day he opened his eyes, he studied the corner of the birthing box—*really* studied it. He sat facing it, then turned to see how his bottom fit in it, then stood on his hind legs to get an aerial view, then lay down and faced it again. Each of these positions lasted only a split second; it was clear his intellect was developing a lot faster than his body.

When Seth took him out for a game of tumble ball, it developed into a game of Examine-to-Determine-Why-Round-Is-Round. Doc Jory turned the ball over and over between his paws, just looking at it and thinking. Seth had better luck playing computer games with Doc Jory. Doc would cock his head and sit with Seth for hours in front of the computer terminal so he could hear the bells and squeaky twings.

Our youngest, the only female, was named Dame Antigone, but came to be called Annie's Ani. She was born a lady, and if that wasn't enough, Annie daily reminded her of it. Dame Ani was gorgeous—the prettiest Saint I had ever seen, and we knew she would become even more so. Even before the pups should have been handled, Annie would sneak into the kitchen and tape ribbons to Ani's ears. By the time Ani walked, she was wearing purple beads around her neck and rhinestones around her paws—thanks to Annie.

Maggie patiently explained to Annie that a pup might accidentally swallow those stones, but when Annie removed them, Ani whined for an hour. Maggie substituted some colored yarns to be wound like jewelry, and that kept the peace for a while.

Winter faded. Patches of ground peeked through melting snow and green shoots reached for sun. Chancey and Maura invented a game following the not-yet-melted spots—sort of a snow hopscotch. Both were quite puzzled when the board game disappeared.

Joseph Cavato came by to do the finish work

inside the shed. He drove a bright red lawn tractor hitched to a small trailer filled with lumber supplies. The tractor looked as if it had been polished, but the wood in the trailer was covered with cobwebs. The trailer was so loaded there had been no room for George.

"Mornin'." Joseph waved.

"C'mon in," Tom yelled back. "Seth and Kathleen are in charge of a major Saturday-morning breakfast."

"That's an offer I can't refuse," Joseph said. He drove the trailer around by the shed and came in the back door.

The pups were already chowing down. Agatha and I got a kick just watching them jockey for center stage. Abercrombie didn't seem to care about his position, though his paw occasionally unseated another unsuspecting pup. Dame Ani would bark, and when the others would look up, she'd move in. Doc Jory liked changing places, as if a new mystery surrounded a single step. Chancey just ate, wherever he happened to be, not the least concerned about the status of his position. Food was food.

"Boy, that sausage smells good," Joseph said, hanging his coat on a back hook. "My dad used to make his own, and it smelled just like that."

Seth filled a plate from the stove and put it down in front of Mr. Cavato.

"Eggs are a little runny," Seth whispered. He pointed to Kathleen and shook his head.

She heard. She turned around. "Over easy, not runny!"

"Won't matter. I got such good news, anything is going to taste good." He took a big bite, then went on. "Loretta is coming back."

The whole family applauded. Maura slithered out of her safety belt and stood in her highchair. Tom lifted her out and sat her on his lap.

"And everything is O.K.?" Maggie asked.

"Seems to be. Dr. Genovese kept her at home twice as long as he thought he would have to, just to be sure she was all right." Joseph cleaned his plate, eggs and all. "He's bringing her here on Sunday."

"Saint Patrick's Day?" Maggie smiled. "That's tomorrow."

"And"—Joseph wiped his mouth with his napkin and folded it beside his plate—"Dr. Genovese wants the O'Rileys to come for the welcome-home party."

"Great," Tom said. "We're due for a happy party."

"But you can come only if you bring something," Joseph went on.

"Grasshopper pies. I'll make two. Loretta will love them." Maggie was thinking out loud.

"That'd be fine, but I meant the Saints," Joseph said. "I spent the first part of this week fixing the fence and a place on the patio where the pups can stay out of trouble."

"But Joseph—" Maggie tried to protest.

"Please, humor us," Joseph said. "George so seldom has his own friends over."

Everybody laughed. Maggie shooed us all outside to help Joseph so she could clean up the kitchen and start the pies.

Joseph worked well with and without an audience. Maura, Annie, the pups, Agatha, and I stayed on the outside of the shed, looking in. Maura had her broom horse and Annie had a pile of baby things that she was trying on Ani.

That beautiful pup sat through it like an angel. When she did look around, Ani seemed to be in search of a camera.

Kathleen and Seth unloaded the lumber and paneling, but not until Seth thoroughly swept the dust and cobwebs and assorted critters off of the trailer. The dust really flew.

Some nails fell into the grass, and so did a peculiar cardboard ball. I'd have to steer the pups away from those nails.

Doc Jory got near enough to examine them, but I pushed him away. His thinking cap was getting too close.

Maura came swinging toward the nails, too, with Chancey at her heels. I stopped her before she reached the nails, but the cardboard round ball went flying when her broom horse hit it.

Chancey watched it fly past him and then watched Maura head toward it. He ran in front of her and began an uncharacteristically loud bark.

Agatha looked up at Chancey. Maura circled around the ball and her stick horse slapped it again. Chancey saw the ball sail through the air and land at his feet. Maura came charging up, and Chancey barked angrily at her.

Chancey? Barking at Maura? Something was wrong.

I heard the hum before I saw anything. A black buzzing cloud was shooting for Chancey's nose. Agatha was right behind me, pushing Maura away.

It wasn't a cardboard ball. It was a wasps' nest! The warm day, the banging around with the broom horse, and the ride in the trailer had awakened the wasps from their winter's sleep.

I did the only thing I could think of. I flattened myself, my hard, thick tummy smothering the gray cone.

It was just a matter of minutes until Tom came up with the hose to drown the stinging wasps. My thick fur had kept them guessing what to bite. Little Chancey had a faceful, and his nose was already swelling. But Maura was O.K.

I wasn't a bit worried about Chancey. Stings hurt, but they heal. Chancey had done what every Saint Bernard sets out to do. He had acted on love.

Chapter 17

Mother Nature sent sixty degrees and sunshine for Saint Patrick's day, so Maggie and Tom assembled a walking troop to attend Loretta's party.

Seth pulled the coach wagon. Its high wooden sides were perfect for holding the pups. Chancey, his cheeks still puffy, but nevertheless in fine form, scrambled to get out and be closer to Maura. Kathleen almost couldn't keep him still until Annie suggested that Maura "go wif the dogs." It worked, though it was pretty crowded.

Tom and Maggie marched first, each carrying a grasshopper pie. Even the whipped cream was green for the occasion, and sugared shamrocks decorated the top.

Annie rode her trike. Agatha and I were the caboose. We could see Joseph and Loretta and Dr. Genovese and Joseph's dad and the other boarders waving and shouting as we came down the hill.

George was wagging his tail. It made us hurry. The closer we got, the more we hurried. Maura decided to stand up to see. Chancey moved to the front of the wagon, too. The weight began to lean to the front. The incline and the weight—I knew we were heading for uh-oh land.

We were just a few feet from the house when the speed and momentum really got going.

I did what any loyal dog would do. I barked a warning.

That's when Tom and Maggie turned around—and stopped.

They weren't fast enough to get out of the way. *Bang!* Everything landed akimbo. Grasshopper-pie grass. Whipped-cream pups. Maura sprouted wings and landed softly in Tom's lap. Maggie's face and hair were covered with funny green cream splotches, and the pups were licking at the tasty goo on her arms and legs. Except Dame Ani. She would carefully dip her paw into